MAXIMUS

and his Mouselings

Brian Ogden

Illustrated by Elke Counsell

Scripture Union

By the same author:
Maximus and the Computer Mouse
Maximus and the Great Expedition
Maximus Mouse
Maximus Mouse and Friends
Maximus Mouse's Christmas Card and other Christmas plays
Maximus Rides again
Tales of Young Maximus Mouse
The Adventures of Maximus Mouse
The Maximus Mouse Primary Assembly Book

Angel Alert!
Aunt Emily's African Animals
Bible Dads and Lads
Ryan the Lion
Short Tails and Tall Stories

First published 2002

Scripture Union, 207–209 Queensway, Bletchley,
Milton Keynes, MK2 2EB, England.

Email: info@scriptureunion.org.uk
Web site: www.scriptureunion.org.uk

ISBN 1 85999 456 3

British Library Cataloguing-in-Publication Data. A catalogue record of this book is available from the British Library.

Printed and bound in Great Britain by Creative Print and Design (Wales) Ebbw Vale.

Contents

Introduction

Jesus, when he was teaching, very often told stories. We call these stories parables. Jesus' parables were simple stories that could be understood by those who heard them. They always started with a familiar situation – a lost animal, a son leaving home and seeds being sown. Each parable contains a single message. Jesus told these stories to make people think and to work out for themselves what God was saying to them. Two thousand years later the situations and the settings for the parables are not always familiar to the children of today. This book retells ten of the better known parables in a contemporary format for use in school assemblies, family services, children's church groups and home reading.

* * *

Scripture Union published *Maximus Mouse*, the first book of Maximus' adventures, in 1991. Since then more than ten other titles have appeared. Between us Maximus and I have written more than one hundred stories and it is now time that we both retired. However, if you see an elderly mouse in your church one day say "hello" – it might be Maximus.

We have had so much fun together and want to say a very big thank you to all those who have made it possible – Elrose Hunter our very supportive editor, Elke Counsell our brilliant illustrator, Scripture Union our publisher and the thousands of children who have made friends with

Maximus. Our prayer has always been that children and even adults will think more deeply about God after reading or hearing these stories.

We dedicate this book to Ailish and Ethan with the hope that they will enjoy these stories when they are a little older.

Brian Ogden and Maximus Mouse

'M' is for mouselings

"Supper's ready, Maximus," said Caerphilly. "Come and sit down, please."

Maximus and Caerphilly are two ordinary mice who happen to live in the vestry in St Michael's Church. Maximus turned off the television and sat down. The meal smelled delicious. Caerphilly was a brilliant cook and ever since their wedding Maximus had always eaten well. Tonight was going to be no exception – it was confetti stew – one of Maximus' favourites.

Caerphilly put the bowl in front of Maximus and the steam from the stew filled his nostrils. He could see the brightly coloured pieces of confetti floating in the thick gravy. In next to no time his whiskers were twitching. He lifted a spoonful to his lips.

"Maximus, I've got something rather important to tell you," said Caerphilly, as she sat down.

Maximus hesitated. The spoon was almost in his mouth, and the first mouse-full was always the best. He who hesitates is lost and Maximus put his spoon back in the bowl.

"Something more important than confetti stew?" he asked whiskerfully.

"I think so," said Caerphilly. "And I think you will think so too, when I tell you."

Maximus looked anxiously at the confetti stew. Was it going to get cold before he had tasted even the first spoonful?

He waited for Caerphilly to continue.

"Maximus, in two weeks' time you are going to be a

VISIT
MOUSEHOLE
MOUSEMAT

father! I'm going to have mouselings."

Maximus was squeakless! He stopped looking at the stew and stared at Caerphilly. He couldn't believe it – he was going to be a dad. He forgot the stew, got up from the table and gave Caerphilly an enormouse hug.

"Careful," said Caerphilly, "mind our babies."

"Oh, Caerphilly," whispered Maximus, "you made me so happy when you married me. Now I think I'm the mousest happy I've ever been."

Maximus did a little dance around the vestry, shouting at the top of his squeak, "I'm going to be a dad, I'm going to be a dad!"

Maximus forgot his confetti stew and raced across the church. He knocked as hard as he could on the Sunday School cupboard door. A rather surprised Patrick opened the door.

"Maximus, whatever is it? Is the church burning down?"

"I'm going to be a dad," squeaked Maximus, as he did another little dance. "Caerphilly is going to have mouselings."

Patrick and his wife Paula were almost as happy as Maximus and Caerphilly when they heard the news. Paula went back to the vestry with Maximus and gave Caerphilly a hug.

"Congratulations," she said. "We're thrilled about your news. I shall start knitting at once."

The two weeks seemed to pass very slowly for Maximus. He couldn't wait to see his first mouselings. He fussed over Caerphilly, brought her organic hymns to eat and even gave her his favourite treat – half baked sermon notes.

At two o'clock one morning Maximus felt himself being gently shaken.

"Our babies are coming," whispered Caerphilly.

Maximus watched open mouthed as first one and then another mouseling was born. The second baby was followed by the third, then the fourth, and moments later by the fifth. There were three boy mouselings and two girl mouselings.

"Caerphilly, they're beautiful," said a very proud Maximus. "I'm sure they're the most beautiful mouselings in the whole world."

As soon as it was light a procession of mice crossed the church from the Sunday School cupboard to the vestry. Patrick, Paula and their forty-three mouselings all came to see the new babies.

"Have you thought about names yet?" asked Paula.

"Yes," said Caerphilly, "the girls are Megan and Molly and the boys are Max, named after Maximus, Magnus and Martin."

Mouselings grow up very quickly and after a few weeks Caerphilly took them for their first day at Mouseling School.

"I don't want to go to school," said Magnus. "Why can't we stay at home and play? School sounds boring!"

"You must go to school," explained Caerphilly, "because there is so much to learn."

"When I was at school we had to learn the three 'M's'," said Maximus. "There was 'M' for Maths – that's all about counting. There was 'M' for Moggies. That's really important because moggies can be very dangerous."

"What's a moggie?" asked Molly.

"Moggies are what we call cats," said Caerphilly. "Cats can be very cruel to us mice and we must keep out of their way."

The mouselings looked serious.

"Dad," said Martin, "what's the other M?"

"It's 'M' for Magnanimouse," said Maximus. "That's a long word which means we should learn to be kind and generous."

"Anyway, come on, or you'll be late on your first day," said Caerphilly. "Don't forget your candle wax chips for break time."

It seemed a long day without the mouselings for Maximus and Caerphilly. They were waiting far too early outside the school for them to come out.

"It was really good," said Molly, on the way home. "I've got ever such a nice teacher and we did a painting and we had a story and we played a game called mousical chairs and I've got a friend called Litmouse."

"How did you get on, Magnus?" asked Caerphilly.

"I s'pose it was all right," said Magnus. "We played pawball and I scored a goal."

They reached home and the mouselings sat down to tea.

"Most important of all," said Maximus, "what did you learn about moggies? Magnus, what about you?"

"I, er, I don't think anyone told us about moggies," said Magnus.

"I don't think you were listening," said Maximus.

"What did you learn about moggies, Megan?"

"I don't think it's nice talking about moggies," said Megan. "I really don't want to think about things like that."

"And what about you, Martin?" asked Maximus.

"Well, it all sounded important," said Martin, "but I can't remember anything because so many other things were happening."

"Oh, dear," sighed Maximus. "Nobody seems to be taking moggies seriously. What about you, Max and Molly?"

"We must always hide when we see a moggie," said Max.

"We must always tell other mice if we see one," said Molly.

"We must learn more and more about them," added Max.

"Well, I'm so pleased two of you listened and learned," said Caerphilly. "Now, off to bed, it's school again tomorrow."

On Sunday morning Maximus, Caerphilly and the five

mouselings were in church for the family service.

"Jesus told a story about a man who sowed some seed," said the vicar. "Some of the seed fell on the path and the birds ate it. Some fell on stony ground and had no water to help it grow. Some fell in the middle of weeds and the weeds crowded it out. Some seed fell in good ground and grew well. Jesus said that people are like that story. Some don't listen to him at all; some don't think about what he says. Some are too busy to bother. But some people listen to Jesus and do what he wants."

Maximus whispered, "Now, I seem to remember some mouselings rather like that!"

Loving Father,
Help us to listen to you,
Help us to think about you,
And help us to grow more like you every day.
Amen.

The Black Paw Gang

"Wait... wait... Now!" shouted Tomouse.

The empty Coke can rolled faster and faster down the roof. It jumped the gutter and fell with a deafening crash on the ground. The old mouse, who had just come out of her mouse hole, was terrified. She dropped her shopping bag and scampered back inside again. Her purse fell out of the bag and lay on the ground next to it.

"Magnus," squeaked Tomouse, "get the money."

Magnus looked at the older mouseling. Tomouse was bigger than he was. Tomouse knew how to fight. Magnus had seen him in the school playground. When Tomouse had asked Magnus to join the Black Paw Gang, Magnus had been over the moon.

"Get the money!" said Tomouse again, this time sounding angry. "If you want to be in the Black Paw Gang you must do what I tell you. She'll be back for her purse any minute."

Tomouse gave Magnus a shove. It was enough to start him rolling over and over down the roof. He just managed to grab the gutter before he fell. He took another look at Tomouse and knew he had to carry on.

Magnus jumped down and looked towards the old mouse's hole. He could hear her on the telephone.

"Please, come quickly, there's a gang of them on my roof," she was saying.

Magnus looked up at Tomouse. He could always run off, but he had to go to school, and there was nowhere to hide at school. Tomouse would find him one break time. Magnus knew what would happen then.

The purse was only a few centimetres away. It had opened as it hit the ground. A five-pound note was sticking out. Magnus tip-pawed over to it. He felt eyes watching him. He looked round. The old mouse had bravely come to her door and was standing behind it. She was ready to slam it if anyone came too near. Magnus looked at the money. He heard more loud whispers from the roof.

"Grab it, Magnus," shouted Tomouse.

"Don't touch that!" screamed the old mouse. "It's all the money I've got!"

Magnus hesitated again. Then he ran to the purse, took the five-pound note, and scampered off as fast as his little legs would let him. As he sprinted off he heard the old mouse shouting after him.

"They'll catch you!" she shouted. "You won't get away with it."

"But we have," said Tomouse, who had crept up behind Magnus. "Well done, Magnus." He took the five-pound note from Magnus' paw. "Now, I think it's time we split up. See you at school. By the way, you won't tell anybody, will you!"

Magnus went back home. When he got there Megan was talking to Caerphilly.

"Next week we're going to sing at the Rodents' Rest Home," she said. "It's brilliant being in the school choir."

"What are you singing?" asked Caerphilly.

"Some of the songs from the Sound of Mousic," said Megan. "My favourite's Idle Mice."

"Where have you been, Magnus?" asked Caerphilly.

"Out... er... just out," said Magnus.

"Time for tea," said their mother. "Come and sit down, please."

"I don't think I want any tea, Mum," said Magnus.

Caerphilly was surprised but she didn't say anything about it until she saw Maximus later.

IDLE MICE
RRH
RRH

“I’m really worried about Magnus,” she said, after the mouselings had gone to bed. “He’s just not his usual self.”

“I know what you mean,” said Maximus, “perhaps we’ll find out more at the Parents’ Evening at school.”

* * *

“They all seem to have settled in well,” said Mrs Nousmouse, the mouselings’ teacher. “The only one I’m worried about is Magnus. I think he’s got in with a rather bad group of mouselings who are not a good influence on him.”

“He does seem different,” said Caerphilly. “I think we need to have a chat with Magnus when we get home.”

“He’s only young,” said Mrs Nousmouse, “and it’s easy to be led by others.”

“I wish he would join the choir like Megan,” said Maximus. “She loves it. Perhaps there’s a group at school that Magnus could join.”

As Maximus and Caerphilly walked back to the church they talked about Magnus. When they got home they found that Magnus was waiting for them. He didn’t look very happy.

“Mum and Dad, I’ve got to tell you something,” he said.

The three of them sat down.

“What is it?” asked Caerphilly.

“I’ve done something really bad,” said Magnus quietly.

And very slowly Magnus told his parents everything that had happened. He told them about wanting to join the Black Paw Gang, he told them about the old mouse and how he had stolen her money, and he told them that Tomouse had threatened him about talking to anyone.

“Magnus,” said Maximus, as he put his paw round his son’s shoulders, “you have done wrong but you have also done right. You did wrong taking the old mouse's money. You have done the right thing because you have told us what happened."

"Friends can persuade you to do good things or to do bad things," said Caerphilly. "Which friends should you listen to?"

Magnus looked at his parents. They were smiling at him.

"I think a good friend would do good things," whispered Magnus.

"Well done," said Maximus. "Now I think we need to sort this out. Tomorrow you and I will go and see the old mouse. You can tell her that you are sorry for what happened. I shall give her the money you took but I think your pocket money might have to repay some of it."

* * *

"Another story that Jesus told," said the vicar, the following Sunday, "was about a woman who made three loaves of bread. The most important part of bread-making is putting in the yeast. It's the yeast that makes the bread rise – without it the bread wouldn't be any good at all. The yeast makes all the difference. You might call it a good influence on the bread. Jesus is the best influence on our lives," he said. "He's the best person to follow."

"Dad," said Magnus, "I think I need some yeast."

And Maximus smiled.

Lord Jesus,
You choose your friends to work with you.
Help us to choose our friends carefully.
Help us to always remember that you are the best friend anyone can have.
Amen.

Rat race

"We're off now," squeaked Molly and Megan.

"Well, just take care, and do what you're told," said Caerphilly. "Don't be late for tea."

"I bet you fall off!" said Magnus.

Megan and Molly got their hard hats, crawled out of the hole in the vestry wall, and set off. From the time they had been young mouselings they had always wanted to ride. They loved the animals and often stayed behind after lessons to groom and feed them. The stables were just down the lane at the back of St Michael's Church.

"What a brilliant day for a canter," said Megan.

"I hope I can ride Nat again," said Molly.

As they got close to the stable they could see there were several mouselings waiting for rides. Megan and Molly knew most of them. There was Tomouse, the leader of the Black Paw Gang. He was boasting to Erasmous, another member of the gang.

"I'll race you," he said, "nobody rides as quick as I do. I'm the best."

Molly saw her friend Litmouse and went over to her. Litmouse was next in the queue.

"Have a good ride," said Molly. "See you afterwards."

Litmouse rode off and Tomouse and Erasmous followed her a few minutes later. Then it was Megan and Molly's turn. Willy Parson, one of the stable mice, led out Nat.

"He's the best rat in the whole stable," said Molly. She threw her arms round Nat's neck and gave him a big hug.

"Come on, Molly," said Megan. "It's time to go."

Megan was already in the saddle on a big old rat called Walter.

"Now, you two," said Willy, "enjoy your ride, but take care." He helped Molly up onto Nat's back and she pushed her paws into the stirrups. "Off you go!"

The track wound gently uphill away from the stable. As they rode higher they could see St Michael's Church in the distance. Soon the track led them into a wood. After the bright sunlight it was dark in the woods. It was hard to see where they were riding. There was plenty of room for the rats between the trees but sometimes the mouselings' hard hats brushed against the lower branches. A squirrel jumping onto a branch frightened the rats. Megan and Molly had to hold on tight to the reins as the rats broke into a gallop.

"Slow down, Molly!" squeaked Megan.

"I'm trying to," Molly shouted back.

The galloping rats raced through the wood, jumping ditches and brushing against bushes. The mouselings clung on. At last the rats slowed down to a walk.

"Let's stop and get our breath back," panted Megan.

"Nat and Walter need a rest too," said Molly. "We'll be out of the wood in a moment then we can stop by the river."

Rats and riders broke out of the wood and walked towards the river. The grass was long and rather marshy.

"STOP!" shouted Molly. "Look, over there."

Megan stared at the long grass. Almost hidden in the grass was a hard hat. Lying next to the hard hat was a mouseling – it was Litmouse – and she was groaning. Litmouse's rat was nearby nibbling the grass.

"Come on, Megan," said Molly. "You look after the rats. I'll help Litmouse."

Molly jumped down from Nat and handed the reins to her sister. She scampered over to Litmouse.

"I don't like the look of her at all," said Molly. "We

must get help."

At that moment Litmouse opened her eyes and groaned again. Molly gently took her paw.

"Litmouse, it's all right," she said. "It's me... Molly. Can you tell me where it hurts?"

"Everywhere!" said the little mouse. "It hurts everywhere, but 'specially my back paws."

"You ride back to the stables as quick as you can," squeaked Molly to Megan. "I'll stay with Litmouse."

Megan jumped into the saddle and galloped off. Molly sat on the ground next to Litmouse.

"It won't be long now," she said. "Megan rides very fast."

* * *

The next day Maximus took Megan and Molly to the hospital to visit Litmouse. She was sitting up in bed. Megan could see that her back paws were bandaged. Litmouse's parents were sitting next to the bed.

"I'm much better – thanks to you," said Litmouse.

"Can you tell us what happened?" asked Molly.

"Well," said Litmouse, "I was just riding out of the wood across the grass when my rat slipped in the mud. He went one way and I went another. I hurt my back paws when I crash-landed on a large stone."

Molly thought about it for a moment. There was something wrong. Then she remembered what it was.

"Tomouse and Erasmous were the next riders after you," she said. "Why didn't they help?"

"Tomouse just rode past me," said Litmouse. "I know he saw me because he shouted, 'Can't stop. I'm winning!'"

"What about Erasmous, then?" asked Megan. "Didn't he see you?"

"He saw me all right," said Litmouse. "All he said was, 'Sorry, can't stop. I must catch Tomouse!' Thank goodness you stopped. I was beginning to think that no one would help me."

CAREFUL!
RATS
CROSSING

* * *

During the family service the next day the vicar spoke to the children.

"A man once asked Jesus: 'Who is my neighbour?' Jesus answered the question with a story about another man who went on a journey. It was not a safe road and before he had gone very far he was mugged. The thieves stole everything he had and hurt him quite badly. A little later someone came along. He had one look at the mugger's victim and rushed by, leaving him there. Not long after that another traveller passed along the road. He had a quick look and didn't stop either."

"I've heard a story like this recently," said Maximus to himself.

"Then a third traveller rode up," said the vicar. "This one did stop. He bandaged the man, put him on his own donkey, and took him to safety. Jesus asked the question that I'm going to ask you. 'Which one of these people was a real neighbour?'"

The mouselings all put up their paws but the vicar couldn't see them.

"It was the man who helped him," whispered Molly.

"Just like the way you helped Litmouse after Tomouse and Erasmous left her there," said Maximus. "I'm really proud of you, Molly and Megan."

Loving Father,
When people need our help:
Make us good neighbours.
When people need our love:
Make us good neighbours.
When people need our prayers:
Make us good neighbours.
Amen.

Really cool!

It was the summer holidays and the mouselings were getting bored.

"There's nothing to do," said Magnus at breakfast.

"Come shopping with me, then," suggested Caerphilly.

"That's boring," moaned Martin.

"There must be something cool we can do," said Molly.

"The coolest place I know," said Maximus, "is the stream!"

The mouselings smiled politely at Maximus' joke. They cleared up the breakfast things and then Molly and Magnus went out.

"I know Dad was trying to be funny about the stream being cool," said Molly, "but it's given me an idea."

"And what's that?" asked Magnus.

"I'll tell you when we get there," answered Molly.

Magnus couldn't persuade his sister to tell him any more. They scampered under the church gate, crossed the lane and went into the field. On the other side of the field was the stream their father had joked about. It wasn't very wide and by this time in the summer was quite shallow.

"So," demanded Magnus, "are you going to tell me now?"

"Well, I think it would be really cool if we made a secret house down here by the stream," said Molly.

"You mean one the others didn't know about?"

"Yes," said his sister, "so we could hide and the

others wouldn't know where we were."

Magnus thought about it. The more he thought, the more he liked the idea.

"Where shall we make it?" Magnus wondered. "It's got to be well hidden. What about over there where all those twigs and rubbish have piled up?"

"Well," said Molly thoughtfully, "that would be OK, but what if it rains? The stream sort of grows bigger and faster. I think the house could be washed away if it rains."

"Good thinking, Sis," said Magnus.

"Don't call me Sis," said Molly, "or you can build it on your own! No, I think the best place would be up the bank a bit. What about that old tree trunk?"

The tree trunk was rotten and had all sorts of fungus and lichen growing on it. It was quite thick and some of it was hollow.

"We could clean this up. They'd never find us here," said Molly.

When they started to clear out the hollow end of the trunk they found it was already occupied. Molly screamed when a huge spider crawled over her.

"GET IT OFF ME!"

"Poor little spider," teased Magnus. "Now you've made it homeless."

The two mouselings worked hard on their secret house.

* * *

"Where have you two been?" asked Max, after lunch. "Haven't seen you all morning."

"That's our business," said Magnus. "We've got a secret."

"Don't say any more," whispered Molly. "Come on, let's get it finished."

When Molly and Magnus left the church they didn't

Test your wings
FLOOD WARNING
2000
1992
1990

see someone following them. It was Max. When they reached the stream, Max stayed hidden in the field under some straw.

"So that's what their secret is," he whispered to himself, as Molly and Magnus crept into the old tree trunk. "They've made a sort of lying down tree house!"

Max stayed for some time watching his brother and sister working on the tree house.

I think two, or maybe three, can play at that game, thought Max. I'm going to find Megan and Martin.

The other two mouselings were watching Tom and Jerry on Rodent TV.

"We've seen this one," said Max.

"Yes, but there's nothing else to do," said Megan.

"There is now," said Max. "I've discovered Molly and Magnus' secret!"

Megan and Martin sat up. This sounded more interesting than old Tom and Jerry cartoons. Max told them how he had followed the other two mouselings and seen what they were doing.

"We could do that!" squeaked Martin and Megan together. "We could build a better house than theirs."

"But it must be a secret," said Max. "They mustn't know we've done it."

"We'll have to go there when they are somewhere else," said Megan. "I know. I'll get Mum to take them shopping."

And that's how Martin, Max and Megan got to the stream without Molly and Magnus knowing.

"Look," said Martin, "over by the twigs and rubbish. They'll never see us there."

The three mouselings started work. They pushed some old cans away from the bank and watched them sink in the stream. They built a little house with the twigs they found caught in the bank. They used a plastic bottle for one side, a rather soggy piece of cardboard for another, and the third was made from leaves and grass.

"We'll leave this side open so we can get in," said Megan.

The three mouselings stood back from their secret house and took a long look.

"They'll never see us here," said Martin.

"Come on," said Max, "it's tea time and the others will be back. Remember, this is our secret, so no telling."

The next morning there were some rather strange looks at breakfast.

"What are you all going to do today?" asked Maximus.

"Nothing much," said Molly quickly.

"Play outside," said Max.

"Well, take care," said Caerphilly. "I think it may rain later."

Max, Megan and Martin were kicking a ball about when Molly and Magnus left the church. As soon as they were out of sight the other three followed them, making sure they weren't seen. Molly and Magnus crept into their tree house.

"This is great," said Molly, "and it's our secret."

At the same time the other three mouselings were creeping along the edge of the stream to their secret hiding place.

"What a laugh," said Max. "They haven't a clue we're here."

As he said that a streak of lightning lit up the sky. Seconds later, thunder grumbled around them. Then the rain started. It didn't just rain; it fell as if someone in the clouds was emptying buckets of water. Minutes later the stream was flowing faster and the water was beginning to rise.

"Just as well we built our house up here," shouted Molly to Magnus above the storm. "The stream's turning into a river."

At that moment Megan screamed at Max and Martin. "My paws are wet. The water's coming in."

She was right. The stream was washing over the bank and the water was pouring right through the middle of their secret house.

"HELP!" shouted Megan. "We're going to drown."

Max and Martin splashed over to the entrance.

"Quick, follow me up the bank," squeaked Martin. "Forget the house – come now!"

You may have heard of drowned rats – well, Megan, Max and Martin were very nearly drowned mice. As they reached higher ground they turned round just in time to see their secret house floating down the stream. By now Magnus and Molly had seen what was happening.

"Come in here with us!" shouted Magnus.

On Sunday the mouselings were in church for the family service.

"Jesus told a story about two men who each built a house near a river," said the vicar. "One built his on a rock but the other man didn't think very hard and built his house nearer the river on sand. One day the river flooded, I expect it was after heavy rains like we've been having. The house on the sand was washed away. The house built on the rock didn't move. Jesus said that those who obey him are building their lives on a firm foundation. Those who don't listen to him are like the house that was washed away – they have no firm foundation."

Maximus and Caerphilly couldn't understand what the mouselings were talking about after the service, but Molly and Magnus seemed to be laughing.

Father God,
Thank you for the wonderful stories that Jesus told.
Help us to learn from them and to build our lives on his teaching.
Amen.

A bad buy

"I shall have to go," said Caerphilly. "My mother, your grandmouse, is not very well."

The mouselings listened to what Caerphilly was saying. It sounded like bad news about their grandmouse.

"We'll manage," said Maximus. "We shall really miss you but you must go and see your mother."

"The best thing," said Caerphilly, "is that you are all good at helping. Magnus, I know you will help Dad with the cooking. You make the yummiest mice pudding I've ever tasted. Molly, you are best at shopping. You know what we usually buy."

The other three mouselings were wondering what their jobs would be. Caerphilly looked at them and continued.

"Megan, you iron better than I do. You're in charge of the washing and ironing. Max, you are the tidiest mouseling and I know you'll make sure that everything is put away, the beds made properly and the rubbish put out. Now, Martin, you are always the most helpful when it comes to cleaning – so you're responsible for the vacuum cleaner and duster."

The mouselings looked at each other. It was going to be hard work whilst their mother was away.

"So," said Caerphilly, "if every mouseling does their job then I'm sure there will be no problems. I hope to be back by the end of the week."

Maximus and the mouselings gave Caerphilly a big hug. They stood by the church gate and waved their paws as she caught the bus to the station. When the bus had disappeared down the hill they went back inside the vestry.

"I'm going to start getting lunch ready," said Magnus. "What would you like?"

"A MacDuck!" said Martin. "We could go out and have a MacDuck."

"I don't think so," said Maximus, "perhaps another day."

"Can we have half-baked sermon notes and candle wax sauce?" asked Molly. "That's my favourite."

"I'd like a hymn sheet sandwich," said Max.

"There was a wedding last Saturday," said Megan, "so if we collect all the confetti can we have my favourite, confetti soup?"

"That's a great idea," said Maximus. "We'll go and get it now. Magnus, you stay here and look up the recipe."

Magnus found the recipe book. It was called Mouse Watering Meals. He soon found how to make confetti soup.

2 cups of mixed confetti
1 cup of water
½ cup of flour
Pinch of salt and pepper
Bring to the boil and simmer for twenty minutes.

Magnus looked in the cupboard to make sure they had everything. One thing was missing – there was no flour. Molly would have to go shopping if they were to have their soup. Just as Magnus closed the book the others came scampering back.

"We've got lots of confetti," said Martin.

"Right, while I wash the confetti I need Molly to go shopping," said Magnus. "We need some flour. Ask Dad for some money and don't be long."

Molly went off to the shops and the others started on

their jobs. Megan checked to see if there was any ironing that needed doing. Max straightened the duvets and tucked all the mouselings' nightshirts under the pillows and Martin started to vacuum the carpet. Half an hour later Molly came back. She was carrying a beautiful red rose.

"I didn't know which flower to get," she said, "but I thought this was the nicest."

"OH, NO!" said Magnus. "We wanted flour – the sort that comes from corn – not the sort that grows in the garden! I can't make confetti soup from that."

"It was a joke," said Molly. "I thought it was quite funny."

The others stopped what they were doing and started to laugh. Slowly even Magnus began to smile. Soon he was laughing with the others.

"Never mind," said Magnus. "We'll make the soup with something else."

Maximus wasn't very pleased with Molly though.

"That's not very clever," he said. "You wasted our money and messed up the lunch. I hope you'll try harder next time."

Every day whilst Caerphilly was away the mouselings worked hard. Magnus did most of the cooking, Megan kept all the family in clean clothes, and the vestry looked very tidy thanks to Max and very clean thanks to Martin. The only problem was Molly.

"Molly, we need some more shopping," said Magnus. "Please buy some Cheddar cheese so I can make a cheese and candle wax pie. We also need a tin of baked beans and some bananas. Please don't forget!"

"I'll get the money from Dad and go on my way home from school," said Molly.

Molly came out of school that afternoon with her friends Polly, Dolly and Chloe.

"I'm going to get some sweets," said Polly.

"Me too," said Chloe and Dolly together.

The four friends went into The Chocolate House. The smell of the chocolate was fantastic. There were chocolate mice, cheese-shaped chocolate on sticks, chocolate covered jellies... in fact chocolate almost anything.

Polly, Dolly and Chloe chose the sweets that they wanted.

"Aren't you going to have any, Molly?" asked Chloe.

Molly looked at the chocolates the others had.

"Yes," she said slowly. "I haven't made up my mind yet."

"Well, come on," said Polly, "I've got to get home or Mum'll be after me."

Molly left the others outside the shop and went back to the church.

"Have you got that shopping I wanted?" asked Magnus. "Come on, I've got to get the pie in the oven."

"Would you like a chocolate mouse?" asked Molly.

"No," said Magnus, "but I would like the cheese for the pie."

At that moment Maximus walked through the door.

"What's the problem?" he asked.

It took some time for Molly to explain that she had not bought the cheese but had bought chocolate instead.

The mouselings and Maximus had a rather strange supper that night – a chocolate and candle wax pie. It was not very popular and neither was Molly.

Just as the mouselings were going to bed the door opened and in came Caerphilly. The mouselings crowded round her.

"How's grandmouse?" asked Martin.

"Much better," said Caerphilly, "and she sends you all her love. Now, tell me how you've got on. I seem to remember giving jobs to everyone."

"Magnus has cooked some lovely meals," said Maximus. "As you can see, Max and Martin have kept our home clean and tidy. Megan has washed and ironed

SALT
RUBBISH
SMALL PEAS
PEAS

all our clothes."

"What about Molly and the shopping?" asked Caerphilly.

Molly looked very ashamed.

"I'm sorry, Mum, but I've let you down."

The next day was Sunday and the mouselings were all in church.

"We're thinking today about another of the stories that Jesus told," said the vicar. "This one is all about using our talents – the things we do best – for God. A rich man gave some money to each of his servants and went away. Two of them used the money to make more money. The third one just buried his money in the ground. When the rich man came back he was pleased with the first two servants – they had used their money well. He was not at all pleased with the third one. God gives us our talents and he expects us to use them. Think about what you can do best. Do you make the most of it?"

"Oh dear," whispered Molly to Caerphilly, "that sounds like me!"

Her mother gave her a hug.

"I know you'll do better next time," she said.

God, our father and creator,
You have given us so much –
The world in which we live,
Our families and food,
Our homes and schools.
In return show us how to make best use of our talents to help other people.
Amen.

Hidden treasure

"Mum, where's your necklace?" asked Molly.

Caerphilly's paw went up to her neck. She felt in her fur. She always wore her gold necklace. Maximus had given it to her on the day of their wedding.

"It's not there," said Molly looking hard. "Are you sure you put it on this morning?"

"Yes, I know I did," said Caerphilly anxiously. "It's the first thing I do when I get out of bed."

"Let's go and check," said Molly.

Mother and daughter walked over to Maximus and Caerphilly's bed. There was a big alarm clock, some books, some other jewellery, but no sign of the necklace. Caerphilly turned down the duvet and looked under the pillows, but there was no sign of the necklace anywhere. Maximus came in as they were looking.

"Maximus," said Caerphilly, "something terrible has happened. I hardly know how to tell you."

"Whatever is it?"

"My necklace, the one you gave me, is missing," said Caerphilly tearfully. "You know how much it means to me."

Maximus put his arm round Caerphilly.

"We'll find it, I'm sure we'll find it. Let's get all the family together and we'll organise a search party."

The mouselings listened hard as Maximus told them what had happened. They all had ideas about where the necklace might be.

"Perhaps it fell off when you were shopping," said Megan.

"Perhaps it's fallen down a hole in the floor," said Magnus.

"Is it caught in your jumper?" asked Molly.

"It might have been stolen," said Martin.

"Perhaps..."

"No more perhapses," said Maximus, holding up a paw. "The only thing we can do is to look for it sensibly. Can you remember where you've been recently?"

"I'm sure I put it on this morning," said Caerphilly thoughtfully. "Then after breakfast I went into the church to find some candle wax and to see if there were any sermon notes in the pulpit. We were going to have sermon note-in-the-hole for supper. Then I came back here to tidy up after the mouselings went to school. It's got to be in the church or here in the vestry."

"Right," said Maximus, in his organising voice, "Magnus and Megan, you two will search the back of the church. Molly and Max, you two will look around the pulpit and the choir stalls. Martin, you will help your mother search in the vestry. I shall look in the other parts of the church."

Magnus and Megan scampered down the long aisle to the back of the church. They hunted through the hymn-books, searched through the service books, looked through the leaflets, and checked out the children's books. But there was no sign of Caerphilly's necklace anywhere.

"All we've found is lots of dust and dead spiders," said Magnus. "I wonder how the others are getting on?"

* * *

Molly and Max scrambled up into the pulpit. It seemed very high when they looked over the top into the church.

"This is where Mum goes on a Monday to get the sermon notes," said Molly. "Half-baked sermon notes are my favourite – they're even better than a MacDuck."

"Well, the necklace isn't here," said Max.

Just underneath Max was a little shelf. On the shelf was a glass of water in case the vicar was thirsty. As he stretched over to look for the necklace Max slipped and fell – straight into the glass.

"Dad, quick!" screamed Molly. "Max is drowning!"

Maximus scampered as fast as he could into the pulpit. There, looking like a rather strange flower in a vase, was Max. He was treading water and every now and then his head appeared above the rim of the glass. Maximus soon pulled him out. Max stood there dripping.

"Max, go home, get yourself dry and change your clothes," said Maximus. "Molly, you come with me, please."

Maximus and Molly continued to search for the missing necklace. They looked on the lectern where the big church Bible is kept. They went into the choir stalls where they found two sticky toffees and an old comic that one of the choirboys had hidden. But there was no sign of Caerphilly's necklace anywhere.

"We'd better go back to the vestry and see if Mum and Martin have found it," said Molly.

Magnus and Megan had just finished and the four of them went back to the vestry together.

"Sorry, no sign of it," said Maximus. "How have you got on?"

Caerphilly was still looking sad.

"We've looked everywhere," said Martin. "In the beds and under the beds, we've searched through all the clothes, and in all the shoes. That wasn't much fun!"

"I just don't know where else to look," said Caerphilly sadly. "I don't suppose I'll ever see it again."

"I'm sure you will," said Maximus. "We'll keep looking."

But the necklace was still missing almost a week later when the mouselings, Maximus and Caerphilly went into church for the family service.

Watermans

"Jesus told a story," said the vicar, "about a woman who lost something that meant a great deal to her. It was one of the ten silver coins, which made up her head-dress. She lit a lamp, because houses in the time of Jesus were rather dark, and she searched hard for the coin."

Caerphilly looked at Maximus.

"That's like us," she whispered.

The vicar carried on with his story.

"She swept the floor, she looked all over her house and at last she found the coin. She was so happy when she found it that she called her friends and neighbours and had a party. Jesus told that story to teach us something rather special about God. When we put God first in our lives he is very happy, just like the woman in the story."

The service ended and the people left the church. Maximus, Caerphilly and the mouselings waited for them to go before moving out from under the seat. Max and Martin started to play a game they had often played before. It was called Push the Kneelers. Kneelers are like flat cushions on the floor. The winner is the one who can push the most kneelers.

Martin placed two kneelers end to end and put his shoulder against one of them. Slowly, very slowly, both kneelers started to move.

"STOP!" shouted Caerphilly. "Look, under there – it's my necklace!"

The necklace was hidden under one of the kneelers.

"Now we know how happy the woman was in the story," said Maximus, "and how happy God is when people search for him and then put him first."

They went back to the vestry with Caerphilly once again wearing her gold necklace and a big smile.

Jesus, friend and brother,
Teach us to put you first in every part of our lives
In our work and play,
With our families and friends,
In our hopes and ambitions.
Amen.

Rhinosaurusses

"Sandwiches, crisps, drinks, cagoules in case it rains, spending money, tissues," said Caerphilly.

The mouselings were going on a school trip. They each had their backpacks open while Caerphilly checked they had everything they needed for the day.

"Now," said Caerphilly, "have a lovely day but please take care and listen to what your teacher tells you."

The mouselings were very excited as they scampered into school. They were all talking about the trip.

"As you know, we are going to the zoo," said Mrs Nousmouse, the mouselings' teacher. "There will be lots of other mice there and it is very important that you stay with me. I don't want any of you getting lost."

* * *

"I've got cheese and confetti crisps," said Molly to her best friend Litmouse. "What have you got?"

"Mum's given me fried ant sandwiches and a chocolate mousse," said Litmouse.

Molly looked out of the coach window.

"I think we're nearly there," she said.

Five minutes later the coach drove into the huge coach and car park at Snipswade Zoo.

"Remember what I told you," said Mrs Nousmouse. "You must stay with me. Now, slowly off the coach and then we'll go and see the elephants."

It wasn't easy following Mrs Nousmouse through all the crowds at the zoo. There were parties of mouselings from lots of schools and one group of mouselings looks very much like another.

"It's... well, it's... just enormouse!" whispered Magnus as he saw an elephant. "I can't believe how big it is."

"It's almost as big as our church!" said Megan.

The mouselings listened as Mrs Nousmouse spoke to them.

"There are two sorts of elephant," she said. "These larger ones come from Africa and those smaller elephants, in the next enclosure, come from India. Some humans think that elephants are frightened by us mice."

Max put his hand up.

"Can we see if they're right?" he asked.

"No, Max, certainly not," said Mrs Nousmouse firmly.

Max looked disappointed.

"Now, it's time to move on to the lions."

The mouselings were even more excited as they got nearer to the lion enclosure. They stood behind the wire fence and looked with open mouths at the five lions in front of them.

"These are African lions," said Mrs Nousmouse. "They are meat eaters and hunt large animals like zebra and wildebeests."

"That's what Dad says you are," whispered Megan to Martin, "a wild beast."

"Yes, but I don't get eaten by lions," said Martin.

"Don't forget to fill in your worksheets," said Mrs Nousmouse, "and draw a lion and a lioness."

Ten minutes later the class moved on again. Next to the lions were three tigers and next to them a large field. In the distance the mouselings could just see a huge creature with a very big horn.

"Can anyone tell me what that animal is?" asked Mrs Nousmouse.

Molly put her paw up.

"I think it's a rhinosaurus," she said.

Rhinoceros
Africanus
Do Not Feed
To the
Penguins
Berg
mouse

Mrs Nousmouse smiled.

"Good try, Molly," she said. "It's actually a rhinoceros. Like the elephant, it's one of the largest animals found on land. Try and draw a good sketch and we'll look it up back in school."

"Please can we have our picnic?" asked Max. "I'm starving. I'm sure I could eat a rhinoceros!"

Mrs Nousmouse laughed.

"I doubt it," she said, "but we'll stop for lunch when you've finished your pictures. We'll go over there by the shop."

The mouselings scampered ahead of Mrs Nousmouse, sat down on the grass, and opened their backpacks.

"Make sure you pick up all the rubbish," said Mrs Nousmouse. "After you've eaten, you can go in the shop with Mrs Greytail five at a time."

Mrs Greytail was the classroom assistant. The mouselings went into the shop in small groups to buy their souvenirs. Magnus bought a plastic elephant, Martin chose a lion, Molly had a rhinoceros, and Megan decided on a book about wild animals. Max came out of the shop licking an orange lolly.

After all the mouselings had been in the shop, Mrs Nousmouse called them together again.

"We're going to see my favourite animals now," she said, "the penguins. Make sure you follow me and don't get lost in this crowd."

Mrs Nousmouse led the way past the shop and along the path towards the penguin pool. There were so many mouselings at the zoo that it got harder and harder to keep her in sight. Martin and Molly were talking about the things they had bought at the shop.

"My lion looks just like the real one," said Martin.

"I'm going to save up and get some more animals to go with my rhino," said Molly.

Martin stopped and tried to see through the crowd.

"I can't see Mrs Nousmouse," said Martin, "but it's all

right, I can hear someone talking."

Molly listened for a moment. She looked worried.

"But that's not Mrs Nousmouse's voice," said Molly anxiously. "That's another teacher. If we follow her we shall get really lost."

"What shall we do?" asked Martin.

Just then they heard a voice they knew.

"Come on, Molly and Martin, we're waiting for you," said Mrs Nousmouse. She had come looking for them.

"Keep where you can hear me," said their teacher, "then you won't get lost."

The mouselings loved the penguins, were scared by the crocodiles and laughed at the monkeys.

* * *

"So what was the best part of the day?" asked Maximus, as the mouselings sat down to tea.

"Seeing the lions," said Martin.

"The elephants," said Magnus.

"I liked the penguins," said Megan.

"The crocodiles were really scary," said Max.

"It was when we thought we were lost and Mrs Nousmouse called our names," said Molly. "But I did like the Rhinosaurusses too!"

* * *

"Jesus told a story about sheep," said the vicar the following Sunday. "Where Jesus lived, there were lots of sheep and everyone knew what sheep were like. Jesus said that sheep know their shepherd's voice. The shepherd calls them by name and he leads them wherever they go. Jesus told the people that he is the good shepherd. If we love Jesus then we listen to him, follow him closely, and he will take care of us."

Molly said, "That's what I meant about Mrs

Nousmouse – when she called our names. Then I felt safe again."

Father God,
Thank you that Jesus is our Good Shepherd, that he knows our names, and that he wants us to follow him.
Help us to listen and to follow him.
Amen.

Plane failing

"Do we have to go home?" asked Martin. "I really, really, really like it here!"

"I'm sorry," said Maximus, "but our holiday ends today. We have to be out of our rooms by 10 o'clock. Now, please go and help your mother pack."

Maximus, Caerphilly and the mouselings were on holiday. They were staying at the Stilton Hotel on the Greek island of Fetta. They had loved every minute of their stay. They could see the waves breaking over the sandy beach from their balcony, the food was mouse-wateringly wonderful, the weather brilliant and everything was right with the world.

Now, not one of the mouselings wanted to go home.

Caerphilly kept pouring sand out of the mouselings' shoes and finding strange shells tucked into pockets.

"Come on," she said, "or we'll miss our plane home. The coach will be here in an hour."

"Can we say goodbye to the sea?" asked Molly. "I mean, can we just go down on the beach again?"

"Only when everything is packed," said Maximus, as he brought five swimming costumes in from the balcony where they had been drying.

"Right," said Caerphilly, "let's do a final check. Max, you look under all the beds. Molly, you check all the drawers. Martin, make sure nothing's been left in the bathroom. Megan, put all these things in the bin. Magnus, you can help your father carry some of these cases to the lift."

There was just time for them all to have a final

scamper on the beach before their coach came to take them to the airport. The flight from Fatwick to Fetta, on Seagull Airways, had been the first time that the mouselings had been in a plane. They had fought to be the one who sat by the window.

"Now, this time you will take it in turns to have the window seat," said Maximus. "No pushing and shoving, thank you."

They came off their coach and joined the long check-in queue. Maximus handed over their tickets and mouseports.

"That's good," he said, as they walked towards Departures. "We're all sitting together in row 1."

"That means when the airmousetress comes with the food we shall get it first!" said Magnus.

The departure lounge was very full – there were mice and mouselings all over the place. Some of them were trying to sleep on the seats.

"Oh, no!" said Caerphilly. "Look, there's a two-hour delay on our flight."

The mouselings looked at one of the screens that gave all the flight details. Caerphilly was right – the screen showed that their departure would be two hours late. It was going to be a very long wait for Maximus, Caerphilly and the mouselings.

* * *

The time went very slowly. They played some games, read their magazines, ate lots of sweets and even slept for a short time. At last they heard an announcement.

"Seagull Airways are pleased to announce the departure of flight 1212 to Fatwick. Would passengers travelling on this flight please go to gate five."

They queued up once again, scrambled on board the bus to take them across the airport, and found their seats on the plane. As the engines got louder and the plane

SEAGULL AIRWAYS apologise for the delay PLEASE AMUSE YOURSELVES
DAILY NEWS
Heatwave in England
BRECON BEACONS

raced down the runway, all the mouselings, together with Maximus and Caerphilly, held paws.

"Bye, bye Fetta," said Megan, who was looking out of the window. "Thank you for a happy holiday."

They had a good flight home and hardly felt the bump as the plane landed at Fatwick. But it was very late by the time they all arrived back at St Michael's Church.

"I don't know what we can do," said Caerphilly to Maximus, as they put their cases down in the vestry. "We should have been home in time to do some shopping. That delay means all the shops are shut."

"Mum, I'm hungry," said Max.

"So am I," added Molly.

"Me too," said Martin.

"I NEED something to eat," demanded Magnus.

"So do I," said Megan.

"Well, I'm sorry," said Caerphilly, "but we couldn't leave anything here while we were away. It would have gone bad by now."

"What about Uncle Patrick and Auntie Paula?" asked Molly. "They'll have lots of food."

Patrick, Paula and their mouselings live in the Sunday School cupboard in the church. They are old friends of Maximus.

At that moment the church clock struck. The mouselings counted as it chimed.

"One, two, three, four, five, six, seven, eight, nine, ten, eleven, TWELVE."

"It's twelve o'clock," said Max. "I've never been up at midnight before!"

"I've never been this hungry before!" moaned Magnus.

Maximus tried hard to hide a smile. But perhaps Patrick and Paula wouldn't mind if he asked them for something to eat, even if it was midnight.

"I'll try Patrick and Paula while you all get ready for bed," said Maximus.

Maximus scampered across the dark church from the vestry to the Sunday School cupboard. He knocked on the door but nothing happened. He knocked louder.

"Whoever it is, go away," said a rather muffled voice. "We're all in bed."

Maximus knocked again. A very sleepy Patrick came to the door.

"Maximus," said Patrick, "couldn't it wait till the morning? It's nice to see you're home but we're all in bed and were asleep."

"Patrick, I'm really sorry to bother you, but please could you let us have something to eat?"

Maximus explained quickly what had happened and Paula, who had come to see what was happening, collected some food. There was half a hymnburger, several slices of bread and some cheese.

"Thank you so much," said Maximus. "We'll show you our holiday photos later."

Patrick shut the door firmly and Maximus went back to the vestry. The mouselings had their snack and went to bed.

* * *

"One day," said the vicar at the family service, "the friends of Jesus asked him to teach them to pray. Jesus taught them the words of the prayer we call the Lord's Prayer – the one that starts 'Our Father'. Then he told them a story about two friends – we'll call them Sam and Jo. One night, very late, Sam had an unexpected visitor. The problem was that Sam had no food in the house to give to his visitor. He thought to himself – my friend Jo will some have food. I'll go and wake him up."

"That sounds like me and Patrick," whispered Maximus to Caerphilly.

"At first," the vicar continued, "Jo wouldn't get out of bed, but because Sam kept on knocking on Jo's door, Jo got up and gave him what he wanted. Jesus told us that we must never give up talking to God. Never stop praying. God loves us and wants to do the best for us."

"Perhaps we could invite Patrick, Paula and their mouselings to tea today?" suggested Maximus.

"Then they could see our photos!" said Magnus.

Heavenly Father,
Thank you that you listen when we pray. Help us to remember that nothing is too small or too big to talk to you about in our prayers.
Amen.

A flying lesson

"Uncle Patrick and I climbed that hill before you were born," said Maximus, pointing with his paw. "We caught the bus to that little village and spent the day walking back home."

"Could we do that, Dad?" asked Megan.

Maximus and the mouselings had climbed up the church tower and were looking out over the countryside. It was a clear day and they could see for miles.

"Tomorrow," said Max, "we could do it tomorrow. Go on, Dad, say yes."

"We could take a picnic," suggested Molly.

"We could fly our kites," added Martin.

"I won't promise now," said Maximus, "but I will ask your mother what she thinks about it. It would be a lovely day out."

They all had another look round and then made their way back down to the vestry.

Magnus ran up to Caerphilly.

"Mum, Dad's got something to ask you," he said. "Say yes – please say yes!"

"I can't say yes until I know what the question is!" said Caerphilly laughing. "Now, give your dad a chance."

"I've been showing the mouselings the view from the tower," said Maximus. "I told them how, before they were born, Patrick and I climbed Outlook Hill. Now they all want to climb it."

"I don't see why not," said Caerphilly. "The weather looks settled. We can take a picnic and..."

"FAN..." said Magnus.

"...tastic!" shouted the others.

* * *

The next morning the whole family was up early. Each mouseling had their own backpack. In each backpack was a can of Dew cola, a packet of Mouse-snax, some candle mint cake for emergencies, and some cheesecake. Martin insisted on taking his kite.

After a good breakfast they caught the bus to the little village which nestled at the foot of Outlook Hill. The hill looked steep.

"Last chance to change your mind," said Maximus.

"No way," said the five mouselings together.

"There's a long way to go," said Caerphilly, looking at the hill, "so don't rush it."

At first, the path leading out of the village was quite gentle. Magnus and Molly kicked a round stone between them as they went along. Martin kept holding up his paw to feel the wind.

"I'll soon have my kite in the air," he said.

As they passed the last cottages the path began to get much steeper and they all slowed down. A little further on, Maximus stopped.

"We'll have a short rest," he said, "and a drink."

They sat looking at the view. Beyond the village they could see a lake with the water shimmering in the sunshine. Behind the lake were more hills with trees on the lower slopes.

"Wonderful," said Caerphilly. "It's all so beautiful."

"Time to put your best paw forward," called Maximus. "We'll stop at the top for lunch."

The path to the top was so steep that no one had any breath for talking. When at last they reached the top they all collapsed in a heap.

"I need mouse-to-mouse resuscitation," panted Maximus.

"When we've got our breath back we'll have lunch."

"Can I fly my kite?" asked Martin.

"After lunch," said Maximus, as everyone opened their backpacks and started eating.

Martin finished first and unrolled some of the kite string. The others lay on their backs, watching him as he ran, the kite above his head. The wind caught the kite and it was soon flying high over the top of the hill.

"Hold on tight," said Maximus, "don't let go."

Martin was now holding the end of the string. Suddenly there was a strong gust of wind. In no time at all, Martin, still clinging to the string, was flying above the hill.

"Help!" he shouted.

"Maximus, DO SOMETHING," screamed Caerphilly.

Martin was, by now, hanging out of reach. One or two birds flew past with very puzzled expressions. They had never seen a flying mouse before.

"LET GO!" shouted Maximus, as Martin soared overhead.

It took several moments before Martin was brave enough to do what his father had told him. By that time he had floated down below the hill top and the others couldn't see him.

"Look, Dad!" shouted Megan, "There's the kite but where's Martin?"

Maximus, Caerphilly and the remaining mouselings scanned the hillside. There was no sign of Martin anywhere.

"Caerphilly," said Maximus anxiously, "take the other mouselings down the path and go home. I shall search for Martin. Ask Patrick to bring a rope and come and find me."

The other mouselings wanted to help.

"No," said Maximus, "the most helpful thing you can all do is to leave me with just Martin to worry about. Now, please go."

SUPERSOAR
KITES

Caerphilly gave her husband a quick hug and led the family down the hill. Maximus started his search for the lost mouseling. As he criss-crossed the hill, he kept shouting, "Martin, shout if you can hear me."

There were little grassy valleys as well as sheer drops on the hillside, but there was no sign of the missing mouseling. Further down, where the ground was more even, a large number of fir trees were growing.

"Martin!" shouted Maximus, again and again.

Maximus stopped. Was that a faint shout? It seemed to be coming from high up in one of the trees. Maximus shouted again.

"MARTIN!"

"Dad, I'm up here!"

Maximus looked harder. He just caught a glimpse of the bright yellow Mousehampton United shirt that Martin always wore.

"Martin, are you all right?" bellowed Maximus.

"I'm stuck," said Martin, "but I think I'm OK."

"Don't move," said Maximus. "Uncle Patrick will soon be here with a rope. Then we can get you down."

* * *

Patrick and Maximus managed to rescue Martin from the tree. There was a very happy reunion when they arrived home safely with Martin.

Paula and all her mouselings were waiting with Caerphilly, Magnus, Molly, Megan and Max.

"Let's have a party to celebrate!" suggested Molly.

And that's what they did.

* * *

"One of the best known stories that Jesus told," said the vicar on Sunday morning, "is the one we call the Lost Sheep. A shepherd is looking after a hundred sheep when he finds that one is missing. He leaves the ninety-nine sheep safe in a field and goes to search for the one that is lost. After looking long and hard he finds it and carries it home. When he gets home he has a party with his friends and neighbours."

Maximus turned to Caerphilly and gave her a big smile.

"Very often," said the vicar, "you and I are like that sheep. We wander away from God. It's then that Jesus comes looking for us. When he finds us, and we find him, God is very happy."

After the service, the mouselings and their parents went back to the vestry.

"Dad," asked Martin, "I don't suppose I could have another kite, could I?"

The look on Maximus' face gave Martin the answer!

Father God,
Sometimes we're like that lost sheep. We wander off on our own, away from you. Thank you that you come looking for us. Teach us to listen for your voice.
Amen.

Rave in the nave

"Look, Caerphilly," said Maximus, who was reading the newspaper, "Rodney and the Rocking Rodents have got a gig at the Town Hall next Saturday. I've always wanted to see them."

"Let's go then," said Caerphilly. "I'm sure we can trust the mouselings for one night. They're quite grown up now."

"It would be fantastic to go out," said Maximus. "I'll get some tickets. I'm sure Patrick and Paula would like to come as well."

* * *

"Have a cool time, Mum and Dad," said Magnus.

"Are you sure you'll be all right?" asked Caerphilly.

"Yes, don't worry about us, we'll be fine," said Megan.

"Just don't do anything silly," said Maximus.

"Bye!" shouted all the mouselings, as their parents went out of the church and down the road.

"NOW WE CAN PARTY!" shouted Max.

Earlier in the week, when they heard their parents were going out, the mouselings had started to plan their party. They collected their favourite CDs, like Willy Robins, Scary Mice and the Rat-Tails. They bought cans of Dew cola and packets of Mouse-snax. And they told their friends. At last the moment had come.

"What about the others?" asked Martin.

"I'll get them," said Molly.

The Daily Mouse
RODNEY
IS BACK
Cheese Shortage

Molly crossed the church and knocked on the Sunday school cupboard door. Percy, one of Patrick and Paula's mouselings, answered.

"Come on, let's rave!" shouted Molly.

Percy and his forty-two brothers and sisters followed Molly into the vestry.

"It's a bit full in here," said Max. "Why don't we rave in the nave?"

The nave is the largest part of the church – where the people sit. The mouselings disco-danced up and down the aisle until they nearly dropped. They drank Dew cola, shook the cans, squirted each other, and then dropped the empties on the floor. They ate mountains of Mouse-snax and kicked the empty bags under the seats. Some of their school friends arrived. The music got louder, the mess got messier, the time got later.

Meanwhile, down at the Town Hall, Maximus, Caerphilly, Patrick and Paula were enjoying Rodney and the Rocking Rodents.

"This is like the old times," said Paula. "Rodney's just as brilliant as ever."

Caerphilly was looking a little worried.

"I hope the mouselings are all right," she said.

"Don't worry," said Maximus, "I expect they're all in bed by now. Ssh... this is my all-time favourite."

Rodney and the Rodents played the opening notes of their number one hit *Your hair is the colour of cheddar, your eyes shine like ripest Edam*. It was the last number on the programme, and Caerphilly had to stop Maximus from joining in.

Back at the church Megan suddenly had a thought. Then she looked at the clock. She gasped – it was nearly eleven – the time Maximus and Caerphilly had promised to be home! Megan scampered over to the CD player. She pushed Magnus, who was the disc jockey, out of the way and pulled the plugs on all the equipment. As the music stopped there were groans and moans from all the mouselings.

"STOP!" she shouted. "You must go home now!"

Everyone looked very surprised. After a lot of fuss and arguing they did what Megan said.

"What's the matter, Sis?" demanded Magnus, looking around the empty church.

At that moment the clock struck eleven times.

"That was eleven o'clock," said Megan. "Mum and Dad are due home NOW! Just look at this mess. They'll never ever forgive us."

At that moment the door opened and in walked Maximus and Caerphilly. They stopped and looked at the church.

"I think it would be a good thing if you all went straight to bed," said Maximus slowly. "We'll talk about this in the morning."

The mouselings walked slowly back to the vestry, their tails between their legs. They got into bed but didn't sleep very well. Maximus and Caerphilly spent most of the night cleaning up the church.

"We must get it done," said Caerphilly, "it's Sunday tomorrow."

"It's Sunday today," said Maximus, as the clock struck one.

Five mouselings knocked on their parents' bedroom door at half-past nine on Sunday morning.

"We are very sorry about the party," they all said together.

"It's nearly time for the service," said Caerphilly, "we'll talk about it later."

* * *

"This is the last in our series on the stories that Jesus told," said the vicar. "The parable we are going to think about today is one of the best known stories. It's often called the Prodigal Son but it should really be called the

Loving Father. Two members of our drama group are going to act out the story for us. They are father and son."

Two men came on stage and stood next to the vicar.

"Dad," said the son, "you know how later on I shall inherit some of your money? Do you think I could have it now?"

The father looked very sad.

"I suppose so, if that's what you really want," he said.

"I'm going away for a holiday," said the son, as he received the money. "It's time I enjoyed myself."

"The father watched unhappily as his son left," said the vicar. "The son went off to a large town where he very soon spent all the money. After a day or two he began to get very hungry. He tried hard to find a job but all he could get was looking after pigs."

"This is terrible," said the son. "The pigs have got more to eat than me. Back at home my father's farm workers have plenty to eat. I shall go back to my father and tell him how sorry I am for what I did. Perhaps he will let me work on the farm with the others."

"So he left the pigs and started on the journey home," said the vicar. "As he came near to his father's house he saw something very wonderful. His father was looking out for him."

"There's my son," said the father. "He's come back!"

The older man hugged his son.

"Father," said the son, "I have let you down. I have behaved so badly that I'm not good enough to be called your son. Please give me a job with your farm workers."

"But his father would have none of it," said the vicar.

"You're my son and you have come home," said the father. "I forgive you for what you've done."

"It truly is the story of the loving father," said the vicar, "who, because his son was really sorry, forgave him for what he had done wrong."

Maximus looked very thoughtful as the humans sang

their last hymn and left the church.

"Mouselings," he said, "I know that you are sorry for what you did and I forgive you."

Maximus and Caerphilly gave each mouseling a big hug.

Loving Father,
Thank you for being just that – our loving Father. Help us to say sorry for the wrong things we do and then to know that you forgive us.
Amen.

More Maximus Mouse books for you to enjoy!

Maximus and the Great Expedition
Brian Ogden

• Join Maximus and Patrick on their great expedition to the Pole!
• Discover Maximus' cure for being bored
• Will the Air Mouse Rescue team get there in time?

More amusing stories about Maximus Mouse and his friends to enjoy at home or to enliven Junior Assemblies.

ISBN 1 86201 939 7

Maximus Rides Again
Brian Ogden

• Join in the excitement of the Great Skateboard Challenge Race!
• Feel the suspense as Inspector Morse Toad investigates a robbery!
• Watch Maximus at the Weight Watchers Anonymouse meeting!

More lively and amusing tales about Maximus Mouse and friends at St Michael's church.

ISBN 0 86201 834 X